Please return/renew this item by the
last date shown to avoid a charge.
Books may also be renewed by phone
and Internet. May not be renewed if
required by another reader.

BARNET
LONDON BOROUGH

K124

To all you bright sparks at Moulsham Junior School! K.G

To Violet M.McQ

TWOO TWIT

by Kes Gray and Mary McQuillan

First published in 2006 by Hodder Children's Books

First published in paperback in 2007

Text copyright © Kes Gray 2006
Illustrations copyright © Mary McQuillan 2006

Hodder Children's Books
338 Euston Road, London NW1 3BH

Hodder Children's Books Australia
Level 17/207 Kent Street, Sydney, NSW 2000

A catalogue record of this book is available
from the British Library.

ISBN: 978 0 340 88211 5
10 9 8 7 6 5 4 3 2 1

Printed in China

Hodder Children's Books is a division of Hachette Children's Books
An Hachette Livre UK Company

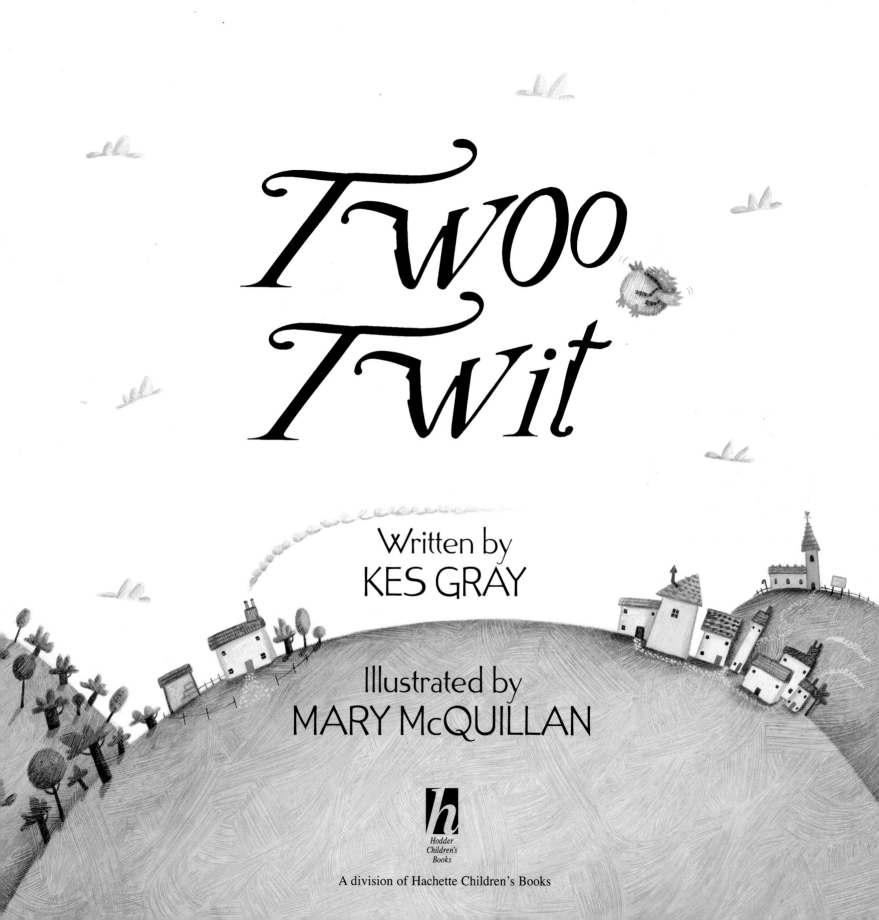

Twoo Twit

Written by
KES GRAY

Illustrated by
MARY McQUILLAN

Hodder
Children's
Books

A division of Hachette Children's Books

Twoo Twit certainly looked like an owl.
He had the eyes of an owl, the beak of
an owl and the feathers of an owl.
But he had the brains of a greenfly!

'I thought owls were supposed
to be clever,' said the fox cubs.
'They are,' said their mum.
'So why does Twoo Twit keep crashing
into his tree?'
'He keeps forgetting the hole is around
the other side,' said their mum.

'I thought owls were supposed to be wise,'
said the badger pups.
'They are,' said their dad.

'Then why has Twoo Twit just perched his bottom on that thorn bush?'
'He hasn't learnt about prickles,' said their dad.

'Aren't owls supposed
to be good at sums?'
asked the leverets.
'Most certainly,' said
the mother hare.

'Then how come Twoo Twit gave the hawk two hundred and fifty blackberries for two beak sharpeners when they were only six blackberries each?'
'Because he's a noodle,' said the mother hare.

'He's a dandelion brain,'
said the weasel kittens.

'He's a mushroom bonce,'
said the partridge chicks.

It was true. Twoo Twit was, without doubt, the silliest
collection of feathers ever to take to the sky.

Every night Twoo Twit's mum would
wrap some rosehip sandwiches up
in a bag and wave Twoo Twit
off to night school.

But Twoo Twit never ever went to school.

Sometimes he would fly to the farm
on the hill to play in the hay bales.

Other times he would fly to the brook
and spend an entire night sending
Poohsticks over the weir.

There were lots of places
Twoo Twit liked going.
Not one of them was school.

Tonight he had decided to go to the church tower to gaze at the twinkly lights of the town. He was hanging upside down from the bell, happily munching his sandwiches, when suddenly ...

He was shaken to the roots of his feathers.

CLANG
CLO
CL
TWOOOOOO!!

'What's happening?' he squawked.

DING

NG

'Make it stop!' he screeched.

DONG

Twit!!

But it didn't stop. It wouldn't stop.
The clangs kept clinging and clonging
and the dings kept dinging and donging.

Finally, thankfully, after two long, long, ding dong hours, the church bell stopped ringing and Twoo Twit stopped wobbling.

With a squeak and a squawk,
Twoo Twit raced back to the forest.

'But couldn't you read the sign?'
said the animals. 'There was
a big sign in the churchyard.'

'Of course I could read the sign,' said Twoo Twit. 'I have better eyesight than all of you.'

'Well if you could read the sign,
tell us what it said then,'
said the magpie chicks.

'Er… it said, THIS IS THE CHURCH,'
guessed Twoo Twit.

'No it didn't,' said the fox cubs.

'THE VICAR LIVES HERE?'
guessed Twoo Twit.

'Nope,' said
the partridge chicks.

'Er… it said, DECENT ORGAN
PLAYER NEEDED,' guessed Twoo Twit.

All the forest children shook their heads.

'It said,
BELL RINGING
CONTEST TONIGHT,'
chuckled the fawns.

'Eight till ten,' giggled
the badger pups.

'Sandwiches provided,'
laughed the weasel kittens.

'You can't read at all, can you?'
hooted the animals.

With the sound of forest laughter ringing in his ears,
Twoo Twit flew home to his mum and dad and hung his
head in shame. He'd never felt such a cuckoo brain before.

The following night a most unusual sound
was heard in the forest. It was as loud
as a church bell and as clear as a choir
solo, but it came from the school.

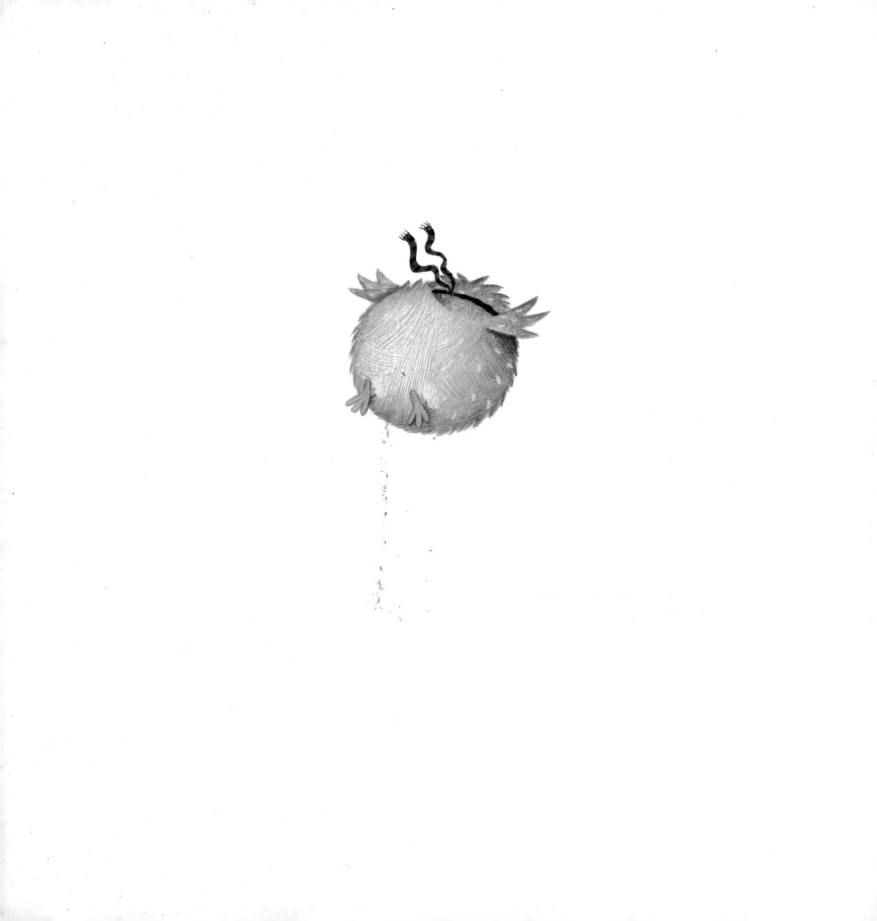

THIS BOOK BELONGS TO:

For Anne (for EVERYTHING.) – L.C.

For my family, with love. x – N.D.

ORCHARD BOOKS

First published in Great Britain in 2018 by The Watts Publishing Group

2 4 6 8 10 9 7 5 3 1

Text © Lou Carter, 2018 • Illustrations © Nikki Dyson, 2018

ISBN 978 1 40835 575 6 • Printed and bound in China

MIX
Paper from
responsible sources
FSC® C104740
FSC
www.fsc.org

Orchard Books, an imprint of Hachette Children's Group
Part of The Watts Publishing Group Limited
Carmelite House, 50 Victoria Embankment
London EC4Y 0DZ

An Hachette UK Company
www.hachette.co.uk

www.hachettechildrens.co.uk

IMPORTANT INFORMATION: ↗
DO NOT EAT!

OSCaR
THE HUNGRY UNICORN

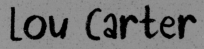Lou Carter ORCHARD 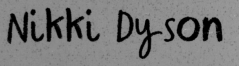Nikki Dyson

Oscar is hungry. But he's eaten

EVERYTHING.

(INCLUDING HIS STABLE.)

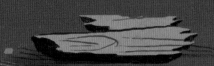

MUNCH
MUNCH

HOME
SWEET
HOME

He'll have to find a new home.

(And something else to nibble.)

This will do
NICELY.

POOF

But the witch doesn't like
Oscar eating her stuff.

(Or her cottage.)

Oscar can't stay on the pirate ship.

CRUNCH!

(NOT NOW IT'S GOT
A HOLE IN IT.)

And the fairies don't want a
hungry unicorn in their meadow.

They say it's not OK
to eat the toadstools.
(NOT EVEN THE TIDDLY ONES.)

Oscar won't be invited to
the dragons' cave again.
The pizzas were meant for SHARING.

And he wasn't supposed
to eat the flashy lights.
(Or the DJ.)

But Oscar is very welcome
at the giant's table.

SLURP!

WHOOSH!

SEND
HELP!
JACK.

GIANT
HOT DOGS

(VERY, **VERY** WELCOME!)

Poor Oscar. Will he ever find a new home?
(AND SOMETHING ELSE TO NIBBLE?)

He's tried EVERYWHERE.

BEWARE TROLLS

Witch's Cottage

YE OLDE PIRATE SHIP

Fairy Meadow

DRAGONS' CAVE

GIANT'S TABLE

(EXCEPT OVER THAT BRIDGE.)

(And trolls **REALLY** like unicorns!)

BUT LOOK!

What a stroke of luck!
Oscar tumbles head over hoof
into Princess Oola's boat.

UNICORN
rescue

Princess Oola has been
searching for a unicorn
FOR EVER.

MARGERY

UNICORNS

WELCOME

TA DAH!

She says that unicorns are the absolute most **WONDERFUL** things in the whole wide world.

(OOLA IS RIGHT.)

Oscar will be happy
here in Oola's castle.

GASP!

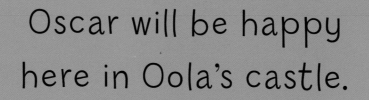

Oola **LOVES** her unicorn to the moon and back.

I ♥ UNICORNS

(And Oscar would eat that too . . .

if only he could reach.)